D1104941

THE CURSE OF RAVEN LAKE

by Chris Kreie

illustrated by Shane Nitzsche

Librarian Reviewer
Marci Peschke
Librarian, Dallas Independent School District
MA Education Reading Specialist, Stephen F. Austin State University
Learning Resources Endorsement, Texas Women's University

Reading Consultant
Elizabeth Stedem
Educator/Consultant, Colorado Springs, CO
MA in Elementary Education, University of Denver, CO

STONE ARCH BOOKS
www.stonearchbooks.com

Shade Books are published by Stone Arch Books
151 Good Counsel Drive, P.O. Box 669
Mankato, Minnesota 56002
www.stonearchbooks.com

Library of Congress Cataloging-in-Publication Data
Kreie, Chris.
    The Curse of Raven Lake / by Chris Kreie; illustrated by Shane
Nitzche.
    p. cm. — (Shade Books)
    ISBN 978-1-4342-0794-4 (library binding)
    ISBN 978-1-4342-0890-3 (pbk.)
    [1. Horror stories.] I. Nitzche, Shane, ill. II. Title.
PZ7.K8793Cu 2009
[Fic]—dc22   2008007991

Summary: Charlie stays at his family's cabin alone. Soon, things get
scary, fast.

Art Directior Heather Kindseth
Graphic Designer: Kay Fraser

1 2 3 4 5 6 13 12 11 10 09 08

Printed in the United States of America in Stevens Point, Wisconsin
072009
005594R

TABLE OF CONTENTS

PROLOGUE
200 Years Ago 5

CHAPTER 1
Alone 9

CHAPTER 2
Under the Ice 15

CHAPTER 3
The Old Man 21

CHAPTER 4
The Animals 31

CHAPTER 5
The Curse 39

CHAPTER 6
Waiting 47

CHAPTER 7
At the Door 53

CHAPTER 8
Darkness 61

CHAPTER 9
Morning 69

PROLOGUE

200 YEARS AGO

A burning sphere lit up the cold night sky. The object dropped through the air and smashed a 50-foot-wide hole through the thick ice that covered the lake.

For an instant, all was quiet.

Then steam began to rise from the open water. It started to boil. The ice around the hole began to melt.

Two dark paws reached out of the hole. Then a black, furry head appeared.

The creature pulled itself onto the ice. It crept slowly toward the shore. When it reached the edge of the frozen lake, it stopped. It flung its head toward the stars.

Then the beast let out a howl, piercing the silence and shaking the trees around Raven Lake.

More and more creatures climbed out of the icy hole. Soon, a group of strange shapes had gathered on the frozen lake.

Finally, one last shape pulled itself from the hole. But this shape was different from all the others.

This one looked like a man.

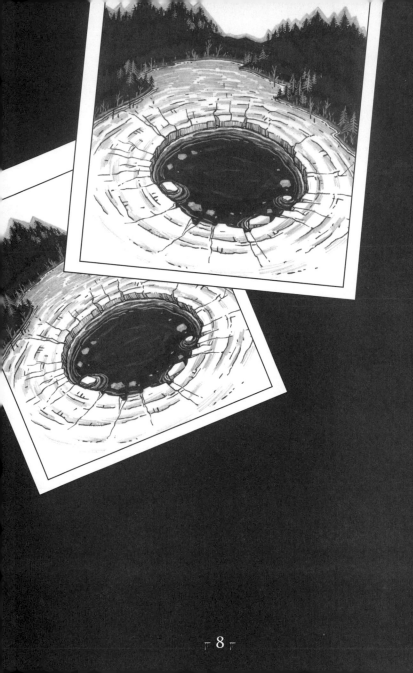

CHAPTER 1

ALONE

The snowmobile turned and headed into the entrance of the long driveway. From behind his helmet's dark mask, Charlie saw the fresh snow. He smiled.

He drove his snowmobile down the hill. He had been planning this weekend for over a year. His mom and dad had promised he could spend a weekend alone at their lake cabin when he turned 15.

No parents, no big brother to boss him around, and no annoying little sisters. Just Charlie, his snowmobile, the snow, and the frozen ice of Raven Lake.

Charlie used an old key to open the front door. He stepped inside and took a long sniff of the musty cedar boards that lined the walls and the ceiling. Then he grabbed his bags from the snowmobile.

After carrying in an armload of firewood, he filled the potbelly stove with birch bark and twigs. He started a blaze.

Charlie grabbed a large metal pot from the kitchen and filled it with snow. He boiled it on top of the stove. Since the cabin didn't have running water, he would use the melted snow for drinking and washing.

He added larger pieces of wood to the fire. He took off his snowmobile gear and sat down in an old leather chair by the stove. The warmth felt great after the cold, two-hour ride on his snowmobile.

Through the big cabin windows, Charlie saw that the evergreen branches were sagging under heavy clumps of snow. The sky was pale blue. The snow on the lake was untouched except for deer tracks that cut across it.

Charlie looked past the nearby trees. He could see the cabin next door. The people who owned the cabin, the Beckers, were an older couple who never came to Raven Lake in the cold weather.

The Beckers spent every winter in the Arizona sun. Charlie wouldn't have to worry about them messing up his perfect weekend.

Then something caught Charlie's eye. Was he seeing things? No, there it was, plain as day. A thin strand of smoke drifted from the Beckers' chimney. Someone was there.

CHAPTER 2

UNDER THE ICE

Charlie frowned. Nosy Mrs. Becker would be over any minute snooping around and asking a hundred questions. The last thing he wanted was company.

He adjusted the stove's chimney, closing it a bit to keep more of the warm air from leaving the cabin. Then he grabbed a bag from the kitchen table and walked out to the shed.

In the small wooden shack, Charlie gathered up his fishing gear – two poles, an ice auger, and a five-gallon pail. He emptied a bag of minnows into a small bucket.

With his arms loaded, he walked through the snow to the lake. It took less than five minutes to use the auger to drill two twelve-inch-wide holes through the thick lake ice.

Charlie was proud of how good he was at using the auger. It was part strength and part skill.

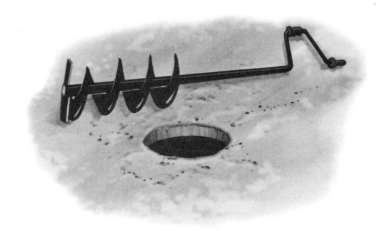

He used to have races with his older brother to see who could crack through the ice first, but when Charlie got too good, his brother stopped competing.

Once he had two lines in the water, the fish started coming.

He could hardly get one shiny, silver fish off a line before the next line was down, having snagged another fish. It was the best fishing Charlie could remember.

He kept any fish that were bigger than his hand. He carefully dropped everything smaller back down through the ice.

He sat on the upside-down pail, watching the lake. With the bright sun overhead, he could actually see a few feet into the water. He wondered just how many fish were down there swimming in the frigid water.

Suddenly, the water went dark. Something was passing beneath the hole. Something huge.

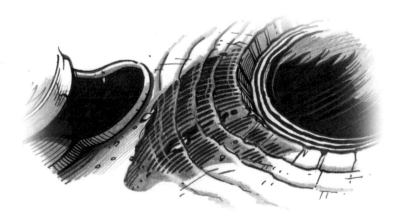

Charlie watched as the dark shape passed by and the water was light again. He felt as if his heart was skipping around inside his body.

Charlie thought he'd missed his chance to see the fish. But then it was back. It wasn't just big, it was gigantic. It was as big as the sea lions he had seen at the zoo.

Things don't grow that big in Raven Lake, he thought to himself.

Charlie watched as the dark object swam slowly underneath him.

Suddenly he felt a tug on his line. He tried to wrap his fingers around the wooden handle of his fishing rod. Before he got a good grip, the entire pole was ripped from his hands and pulled through the ice. Charlie blinked. His fishing rod was gone.

CHAPTER 3

THE OLD MAN

Charlie sat at the campfire next to the lake. He ate some fish, which he had cleaned, breaded, and fried. More fish were sizzling in the frying pan, turning a delicious golden brown.

As Charlie gobbled down the salty fish, he looked out at the lake. He couldn't stop thinking about the shadow he had seen under the ice. It must have been a northern pike, or maybe even a muskie.

Charlie had seen pictures of muskies that were as big as grown men. But Raven Lake didn't have any muskies. Then how could he explain his missing fishing rod?

The sun was still shining, but it was creeping closer to the horizon. Within an hour, it would drop below the trees on the other side of the lake.

Charlie looked down at his paper plate. Only a few crumbs and bones were left. He flicked them into the trees. Then he tossed his plate and napkin into the fire and watched them go from white to black.

He dunked the frying pan in some snow to cool it down. Then he collected the other cooking supplies in his arms.

Charlie was about to walk back to the cabin. A noise behind him made him stop.

Something was moving behind the trees. At first, Charlie wasn't sure what he was seeing. It looked like a weird gray blob moving in the snow.

When he looked closer, Charlie could see that the blob was actually a group of rodents. They were fighting over the scraps he had thrown away.

The ugly little things had bald, skinny tails and flat, upturned noses. Their long gray hair hung to the ground, covering their legs and feet.

Charlie had never seen creatures like them before. They were hissing and clawing at one another. The larger ones snarled, showing their sharp white teeth.

"Strange little things, aren't they?" someone said.

Charlie jumped. He turned around.

An old man with plaid overalls was standing by the fire. His bony white hands stuck out from his sleeves, and an orange hunting cap covered his head. Charlie had never seen the man before.

Charlie froze. His heart thumped in his chest.

"I said, strange little things, huh?" the man said, louder.

"Uh, yeah," Charlie replied quietly.

"Do you know what they are?" asked the man.

"No," said Charlie. "Do you?"

"No, I don't," the old man said. He was staring directly into Charlie's eyes. It gave him the creeps.

Charlie looked away. The man had scared the life out of him, sneaking up like that. But it was just an old man. Nothing to be afraid of.

"Great fishing today," said Charlie, making eye contact once again. "I caught seven fish in less than an hour."

"Is that right?" said the old man.

Charlie tried to smile. "Yep. Have you been fishing at all?" he asked.

"Nope," the old man said. "Not a lick."

Charlie looked down at his boots. Something about the conversation was making him nervous. "Well, I better be going," he said.

"You seen anything else funny lately?" asked the old man.

"Funny?" asked Charlie.

"Yeah. Did you see any other strange animals since you got here?" the old man asked, grinning a weird little smile.

"No," said Charlie. "Not really." He paused and took a look out at the lake. "Well, there was this huge fish."

The old man's eyes lit up. "Aha!" he said.

"It was just a fish," Charlie said quickly. "No big deal."

The old man laughed. His eyes were locked on Charlie's.

"Just a fish," the man said.

He spit some brown juice into the snow. Some of the juice dribbled down his chin. Then he said, "Well, son. If those are the strangest animals you see tonight, consider yourself lucky." He wiped his chin with the back of his hand.

"What do you mean?" asked Charlie.

The old man looked away for the first time. "Your friends are gone," he said, pointing to the trees.

Charlie turned around. The gray blob had vanished. He walked over to the edge of the trees and bent down. Something was still there.

One of the strange rodents was lying motionless in the snow. A little blood trickled from its mouth.

Charlie stood up and looked behind him. The old man was walking away, toward the Beckers' cabin.

"Who are you?" shouted Charlie. "What's going on here?"

The old man kept walking.

"What's going on?" Charlie shouted again.

The man turned his head and stared at Charlie. Then he said, "It's the curse of Raven Lake, son. And there ain't a darn thing you can do about it."

CHAPTER 4

THE ANIMALS

"The curse of Raven Lake," Charlie said, laughing. His hands were buried in a tub of soapy water. He was back in the cabin, finishing up the dishes. Rinsing the frying pan in another tub of clean water, he added, "Crazy old man."

Deep down, though, Charlie was a little spooked. The creepy old man had made him nervous.

He thought about hopping on his snowmobile and heading home. But night was coming fast, and the ride would take twice as long in the dark.

Plus, what would he tell his older brother? That he had come home early because he was afraid of a big fish and some ugly rats?

No way. He was staying.

Charlie placed the pan in the dish rack, then dried his hands on a kitchen towel. He carried the tub of dirty water to the door and tossed it outside.

Looking out across the snow, he noticed some long shadows on the lake.

"Deer," he said to himself. "Just some deer."

Charlie found a pair of binoculars in his bag. He went to the window and focused the binoculars on the five deer that were crossing the lake.

They were dull gray, not the copper color they would become in the summer. But they were still beautiful. Charlie figured they were heading to the creek that emptied into Raven Lake. The deer were probably just looking for drinking water.

Charlie calmed down and felt less scared as he watched the deer.

Suddenly, the deer stood still. They all stared to the right. Charlie watched them, wondering what they were looking at. It seemed like they were scared.

He put the binoculars down so he could get a view of the entire lake. That's when he saw them. Two other animals crept out from the trees that bordered the lake. They headed toward the deer.

Wolves, Charlie thought.

With the binoculars back to his eyes, he looked more closely at the animals. Their legs were long and athletic. But their fur, instead of being bristly, like a dog's, was curly and solid black. Their heads were huge, much bigger than wolves' heads.

They weren't wolves at all. Charlie had never seen animals like them before.

Charlie looked back at the deer. Their heads turned nervously from side to side. Then he saw why. Three more of the large, black creatures were walking toward the deer from the other side.

One of the strange animals lifted its head and howled. In a quick burst, the deer fled across the lake.

The black beasts followed. The beasts struggled in the deep snow, because they were lower to the ground than the deer were.

Charlie stared at the scene in front of him. His hands shook from fear and excitement. He cheered silently for the deer.

They escaped from the other creatures and disappeared into the dark evergreens across the lake.

The black creatures gathered in a pack. Slowly, one by one, the creatures stood up on their hind legs. Like humans.

The pack sprinted toward the trees. Following the tracks made by the deer, they disappeared into the forest.

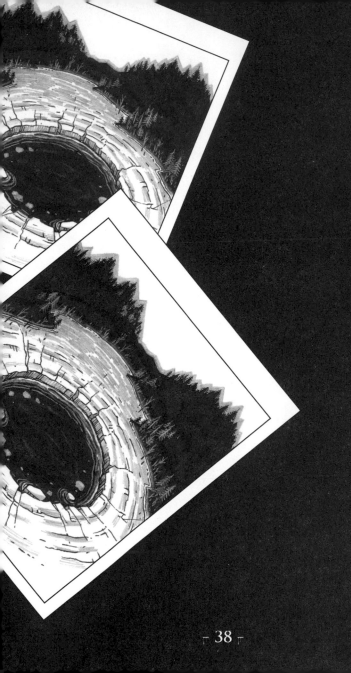

CHAPTER 5

THE CURSE

Charlie crashed through the trees as he ran toward the Beckers' cabin. He was scared, but more than that, he needed to get some answers. He had never seen so many strange things in the woods. He needed to find out what was going on.

The thing under the ice, the killer rodents, and now these wolf-like creatures. Something strange was going on. The old man knew something. Charlie was going to make him talk.

As he got close to the edge of the Becker house, he quickly stopped. The old man was walking slowly up the driveway.

Charlie was about to yell when he noticed that the old man was walking backward. He was dragging something behind him.

Charlie squatted down in the snow behind some skinny birch trees. Even though night was nearly upon Raven Lake, he could see what the man was dragging.

It was the same kind of animal Charlie had just seen chase after the deer. It wasn't moving. It looked stiff, maybe frozen.

The man pulled the lifeless creature up the driveway and into the Beckers' shed. Charlie stared. Fear crept deep into his chest.

The old man appeared from the shed. He saw Charlie, but he turned his back and began to lock the shed door.

"What's going on around here?" Charlie demanded. He hoped that he sounded more angry than scared.

The old man turned to look at him, but didn't say anything.

"I said, what's going on around here?" Charlie repeated. "I deserve some answers."

The old man laughed. "I don't have any answers," he said. He kicked the snow off his boots. "But I do have a story I could tell you," he added.

The old man spit into the snow. Charlie looked down and wrinkled his nose.

"Would you care to hear the story?" asked the man.

Charlie didn't feel like he had a choice. "Go ahead," he said.

"As a matter of fact, this is a story I first heard when I was about your age," said the man. He spit into the snow again.

Then he said, "Raven Lake is cursed. Just like I told you before. No one knows for sure how long it's been cursed or exactly how it happened. But the story goes, every 25 years, on the night of the year's first full moon, something happens to this lake. Something wrong."

Charlie could feel his heartbeat gaining speed. The man went on, "Things come out of the woods. Strange things, ugly things, awful things. You've seen them. They wander around the lake, feeding. Then, after 24 hours, they disappear. They don't come back for another 25 years. You picked the wrong time for a trip to the lake, kid."

The old man stepped toward the Beckers' cabin.

"There's something in the shed," Charlie said. "I saw it. Tell me what it is."

The man stepped onto the cabin porch. He turned the doorknob and opened the door.

"I saw it on the lake. I saw it stand up," Charlie shouted. He took a few steps toward the man. His bravery shocked even him.

"You need to tell me how to stop them!" Charlie yelled.

The old man chuckled. Then he looked at Charlie and said, "Son, go home and lock your doors. Get into your bed, close your little eyes, then hope with everything you have that you'll see the sun again. You can't stop the curse of Raven Lake!"

The door slammed shut behind him.

⊤ CHAPTER 6 ⊤
WAITING

Back in the cabin, Charlie's mind was racing. He couldn't call home. The cabin didn't have a phone. And he couldn't get reception for his cell phone this deep in the woods.

He would have to ride more than a mile back to the main road before his phone would work. Once he was that far, he might as well just keep going. But it was already pitch black outside.

If he had a car and could drive, he would risk it. But on his snowmobile, there was no way. He would be in the open, easy prey for anything hiding in the dark.

The safest place, Charlie decided, was in the cabin. If the doors and windows were locked, what could happen? It would be a scary night, that's for sure. But just like the old man had said, once he survived the night, everything would be okay.

Charlie pushed a couch in front of the sliding glass door. He looked out toward the lake. Everything was dark.

Charlie glanced at the clock. It was 7 p.m. The sun wouldn't rise for another twelve hours.

He turned off all the cabin lights. Darkness inside would make it easier to see into the darkness outside.

Charlie grabbed a thick blanket and sank onto the couch. He had a good view out the window. When his eyes got used to the night, he could see a full moon and a clear sky, lit up with stars.

Wrapped in the blanket, Charlie waited.

Everything was so quiet, so still. He kept picturing the black beasts. He kept thinking about the dead rodent, the giant fish, and the strange old man.

What would he do if he saw something outside? What could he possibly do if a creature crashed through the window?

For a second, he wished it would happen. Part of him wanted something noisy and active to break the stillness. At least he would get it over with.

Charlie shook his head. He didn't know which would be worse — facing one of those creatures, or waiting in the cabin, letting his thoughts drive him crazy.

He didn't think he could sit there much longer.

Charlie took several deep breaths. After a few minutes, he started to calm down.

He thought about the weekend, and how he had wanted it so much. "Be careful what you wish for," he whispered.

Coming to the cabin alone had been a mistake, he realized. He had wanted to prove himself to his parents, to show that he was becoming an adult. But now, more than ever, he felt like a little kid.

Charlie stared out at the lake. He scanned around from right to left then back again. He lost track of time as he moved his head from side to side very slowly. Soon his eyes felt heavy. It was difficult to keep his head up. Charlie took one last look at the lake. Then he fell asleep.

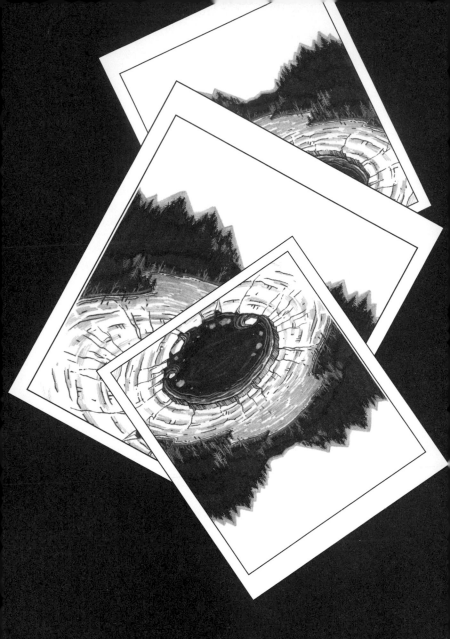

CHAPTER 7

AT THE DOOR

A sudden noise woke Charlie. He quickly sat up. It took several seconds for his eyes to focus in the darkness and for him to remember why he was lying on the couch in the middle of the cabin's living room.

His watch read 9:45. Charlie sighed. The night had barely begun.

He stared out toward the lake.

Nothing was out there. No old man. No animals. No scary creatures howling in the moonlight.

Silence wasn't unusual in January. In the summer at this time of night, he'd be hearing owls, or loons, or frogs. But the winter was different. The winter was always really quiet at Raven Lake.

But he had heard something, right? Something had woken him up.

Charlie stretched out on the couch and pulled the blanket up to his chin. He closed his eyes and rolled onto his side. He was just about to drift away to sleep when he heard the noise again.

His eyes shot open. He waited. He held his breath. After a few more seconds, he heard it again.

Scratching.

Charlie lay still on the couch, hoping the noise would go away. But it didn't.

Scratch. Scratch. Scratch.

The sound was coming from the other end of the cabin. Something was scratching at the front door.

Charlie slowly got to his feet. The air in the cabin was cold, because the fire in the stove had nearly gone out.

Still, Charlie could feel sweat beading up on his forehead. He was tempted to look out the front window to see what was scratching at the door, but he wasn't sure he wanted to find out.

"Okay," Charlie said. "Calm down."

The scratching didn't stop. Charlie wondered frantically how many creatures were out there.

It sounded like a pack. He thought about the five black beasts he had seen chase the deer across the lake.

His nerves were on fire. He had to keep moving.

Suddenly, there was a new sound. Charlie looked up at the ceiling. Something was on the roof.

Charlie waited silently in the middle of the living room. The sound on the roof continued. It was hard to notice unless you stayed still and listened for it. *Pat, pat, pat.* It was definitely there.

Charlie's heart was galloping. He took some deep breaths, but his chest felt like it was locked up.

He sat down and put his head in his hands, trying to calm down.

"Breathe. Just breathe," he told himself.

Charlie tried to think, tried to come up with a plan. But the image of creepy monsters outside the cabin ran through his mind.

After a few minutes, he knew he had no choice. "If I stay here, I'm dead," he whispered.

Charlie jumped to his feet. He raced through the kitchen to the back pantry, a small room full of canned food. A large freezer stood in the back of the room. Charlie lifted the freezer's heavy lid.

Just like he'd remembered, the freezer was full of several large items wrapped in white paper. Charlie reached in and grabbed as many as he could carry.

Last November, Charlie and his dad had shot two large deer during deer hunting season. At the time, Charlie would never have imagined how he'd be using the meat.

He dumped the frozen meat on the kitchen floor. Then he quickly unwrapped each package. He grabbed the garbage can and dragged it to the center of the floor. He picked up the frozen meat and tossed it into the can.

Charlie crept over to the front door. The scratching seemed to have gotten louder. He found his snowmobile key. Then he put on his snow pants and coat.

"Okay, monsters of Raven Lake," said Charlie as he dragged the garbage can through the living room. "Ready to eat?"

Charlie stood by the sliding glass door that led out to the lake. He sucked in some air. "This is either really brilliant or really stupid," he said. He took another deep breath and flung open the sliding door.

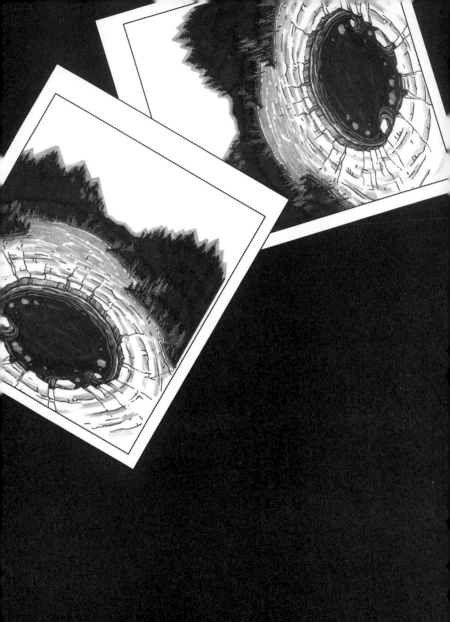

CHAPTER 8

DARKNESS

"Come and get it, whatever you are!" Charlie shouted into the night. He flung the frozen meat as far into the yard as he could.

Quickly, he slammed the sliding door shut. Then he watched through the glass as several large shapes quickly swarmed around the meat. The scratching on the front door and the footsteps on the roof had stopped.

It was his only chance. Charlie ran out the front door of the cabin and rushed to his snowmobile. He hopped on, his shaking fingers searching for the ignition in the dark.

Suddenly he felt the cold on his head. He had forgotten his helmet inside. It was too late to go back. He would have to ride without it.

Charlie fired up the engine and sped up the hill, away from the cabin. It wasn't until he reached the end of the driveway that he had the courage to look behind him.

Darkness. Nothing else.

As Charlie turned his snowmobile onto the lake road, he gunned the engine and took off. He thought about home, about people, about his family. He couldn't wait to see them.

He would stop at Billy's Store once he got to the main road. He'd call his parents. He would tell them he was on his way home.

His parents would think he was crazy, and he'd have a lot of explaining to do. But at least he'd be alive.

Then he heard a howl. It was the same sound he had heard earlier from the beasts across the lake. But this time it was much louder, much closer.

Charlie sped up.

He turned a sharp corner. He was flying, going faster than he should've been.

As he rounded another turn in the road, he saw something standing directly ahead of him. It was huge. It was at least the size of a moose, but it gleamed as white as a ghost.

Charlie swerved to avoid it, but the road was too narrow. He lost control of his snowmobile and flew over a bank of snow.

Suddenly, he slammed his head into a low tree limb. As he screamed, he was thrown from the snowmobile.

A few seconds passed. Charlie struggled onto his hands and knees. His head throbbed with pain. There was something warm and sticky on his face. Was it blood?

He crawled to his snowmobile. The engine was smoking. The frame was banged up pretty bad. Charlie could smell gasoline.

Then he remembered the howling, and the enormous shape that had forced him off the road. He needed somewhere to hide, fast.

It was hard to think clearly. His head felt like it was about to split open. And his heart was speeding like a rabbit's.

Finally, Charlie saw a large pine, which had fallen over in a previous storm. Underneath a portion of the enormous tree, Charlie could see a dark hole, where the roots had once rested deeply in the ground.

Charlie dropped down and stuffed himself into the hole. Once he was inside, he reached out and pulled in handfuls of snow to cover up his hiding place.

He held his breath and listened. The forest was quiet. Finally, he curled into a ball and drifted off to sleep.

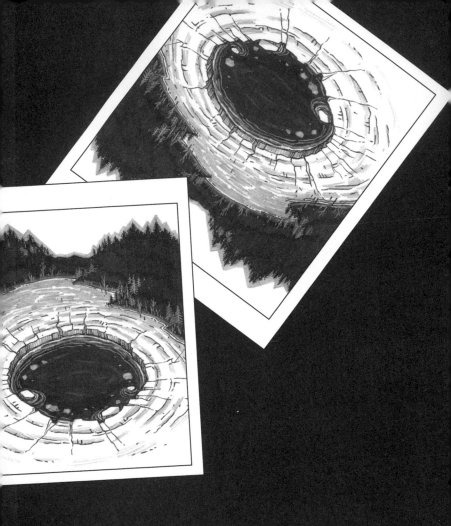

CHAPTER 9
MORNING

The next thing Charlie saw was a
narrow band of sunlight, shining through
a hole in the snow. He pushed through
the snow, back into the outside world.
The sun was shining through the trees.
It was morning.

His head still throbbed. The pain of his injury, and the memories of the night before, shot through his body like an electrical current. But Charlie knew he had to figure out what had happened during the night.

He scanned the ground for tracks from the animal that had forced him off the road. A layer of new snow had fallen during the night, so he couldn't see anything.

When Charlie made his way back to the Beckers' cabin, he found the door locked. There was no sign of the old man, no smoke coming from the chimney, no tire tracks in the driveway.

Had it all been a dream?

He ran to his own cabin. The raw meat was gone. There was nothing left to prove what had happened last night.

Then Charlie remembered.

He ran to the front of the cabin. There, on the door, was all the proof he needed. It may not be enough to convince his family, but it was enough for Charlie.

The door was covered with long, deep scratches. Scratches from the creatures that had tried to claw their way into the cabin.

The curse was real.

"Twenty-five years," he said aloud, remembering what the old man had said.

Charlie looked out toward Raven Lake. It seemed so calm.

Then he noticed the tracks.

Large pawprints, tiny claws, hoofprints, and slithering trails. They all led to the middle of the lake. Charlie followed them onto the ice. In the center of Raven Lake, the tracks gathered together in a tight circle. And there, in the middle of them, Charlie saw tracks left behind by something else. They were human footprints.

About the Author

Chris Kreie's family has owned a cabin on a lake in Minnesota's north woods since he was a young child. He loves spending time there, but sometimes he still gets spooked by things that go bump in the night. Chris lives in Minnesota with his wife and two children. He works as a school librarian, and in his free time he writes books like this.

About the Illustrator

Shane Nitzsche has been creating artwork since he could wrap his little fingers around a pencil, but he really started to take it seriously after he cracked open his first comic book. Shane spent his younger years in rural Missouri, but has since moved to Portland, Oregon and can't think of any better place in the world to continue pursuing his career. (Oh, and that last name? It's pronounced NIT-chee.)

Glossary

binoculars (buh-NOK-yuh-lurz)—an instrument that you look through with both eyes to make distant things seem nearer

bravery (BRAYV-ur-ee)—if you have bravery, you are showing courage and not fear

creature (KREE-chur)—a living being, human or animal

curse (KURSS)—an evil spell

ice auger (EYESS AWG-ur)—a tool used to drill a hole into a frozen lake so that you can fish

object (OB-jikt)—something that you can touch but that is not alive

rodent (ROHD-uhnt)—a mammal with large, sharp front teeth

snowmobile (SNOH-moh-beel)—a vehicle used to travel over snow

sphere (SFEER)—a solid, round shape (like a basketball or a globe)

Discussion Questions

1. Who was the old man in this book? What was he doing at Raven Lake?

2. What do you think the creepy animals were in this book? What did they do at the end of the book?

3. Do you think Charlie should have gone to Raven Lake alone? Why or why not?

Writing Prompts

1. Charlie was excited about spending a weekend alone at his family's cabin. If you could spend a weekend doing whatever you wanted, what would you do?

2. Imagine that you are Charlie. Write a letter to one of Charlie's friends, telling him or her about the night at Raven Lake.

3. Charlie decides to try to escape on his snowmobile. What do you think would have happened if he'd stayed at Raven Lake? Write about it!

MORE SHADE BOOKS!
Take a deep breath and

One boring summer day, Emily decides to get out her dad's old camera. When she develops the pictures in the darkroom, she finds an extra photograph. The next day, the photograph comes true in a horrifying way.

Step into the shade!

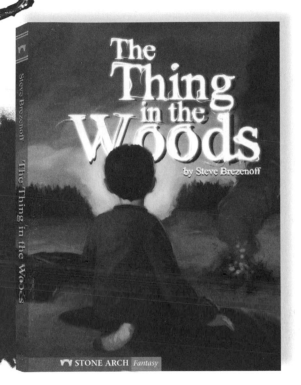

The Thing in the Woods

by Steve Brezenoff

Steve Brezenoff

The Thing in the Woods

▼▼ STONE ARCH *Fantasy*

Jason and his dad have car trouble in the desert. They decide to camp overnight. Before they go to sleep, Jason's dad tells him a creepy story. When Jason wakes up, his dad is missing! It seems as though the ghost story is coming true!

Internet Sites

Do you want to know more about subjects related to this book? Or are you interested in learning about other topics? Then check out FactHound, a fun, easy way to find Internet sites.

Our investigative staff has already sniffed out great sites for you!

Here's how to use FactHound:

1. Visit *www.facthound.com*

2. Select your grade level.

3. To learn more about subjects related to this book, type in the book's ISBN number: **9781434207944**.

4. Click the **Fetch It** button.

FactHound will fetch the best Internet sites for you!